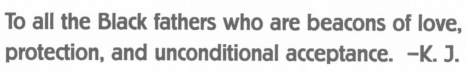
For every child who's learned to ride a bike and for those who will one day learn. —V. B.

To all the Black fathers who are beacons of love, protection, and unconditional acceptance. —K. J.

Text copyright © 2022 by Valerie Bolling.
Illustrations copyright © 2022 by Kaylani Juanita.

Library of Congress Cataloging-in-Publication Data available.

ISBN 978-1-7972-1248-7

Manufactured in Canada.

Design by Lydia Ortiz and Aya Ghanameh.
Typeset in Berliner Grotesk.
The illustrations in this book were rendered in mixed media (scanned textures/paper) and digitally.

10 9 8 7 6 5 4 3 2 1

Chronicle books and gifts are available at special quantity discounts to corporations, professional associations, literacy programs, and other organizations. For details and discount information, please contact our premiums department at corporatesales@chroniclebooks.com or at 1-800-759-0190.

Chronicle Books LLC
680 Second Street
San Francisco, California 94107

Chronicle Books—we see things differently. Become part of our community at www.chroniclekids.com.

Together We Ride

Written by **Valerie Bolling**

Illustrated by **Kaylani Juanita**

chronicle books·san francisco

Inside

Outside

Slow . . . guide

Quick stride

Slip,

slide,

tossed aside

Hug-cried

Tears dried

Decide . . .

Push,

goodbyed

FLY!

Pump,

Run beside

Coast, glide

Inside

Outside

Side by side

RIDE!